An Evil Motherhood

Fabulous Novellas

An Evil Motherhood

(An Impressionist Novel)

by

Walt Ruding

Illustrated by Aubrey Beardsley

Skomlin
House of Memory

Skomlin
House of Memory and Imagination
For more information visit *www.skomlin.com*

A Skomlin Book
Melbourne, Australia

First published London 896
© Skomlin, 2017

ISBN: 978-0-6482388-5-0 *(paperback)*
ISBN: 978-0-6482388-6-7 *(eBook)*

 A catalogue record for this book is available from the National Library of Australia

The paper used in this publication meets the minimum requirements of ANSI/NISO Z39.48-1992 (R1997) (Permanence of Paper). The paper used in this book is from responsibly managed forests. Printed in the United States of America, the United Kingdom and Australia by Lightning Source, Inc.

Le coup dont tu te plains t'a préservé peut-être,
Enfant ; car c'est par là que ton coeur s'est ouvert.
L'homme est un apprenti, la douleur est son maître,
Et nul ne se connaît tant qu'il n'a pas souffert.

Alfred de Musset

A PREFATORY NOTE

My prefatory words shall be few, and relevant rather than graceful. As to myself, then- -Nothing. How I learnt or invented my story will not interest the reader; enough that, had it the artistic misfortune to be "founded on facts," I should seek to redeem it with all the resources of Fiction.

Nature is often sensational in effects the significance of which we are unable to ignore. Some may barely tolerate such sensation; some hanker after comic relief or the restful padding of a love interest; perhaps but a few will understand a tragedy disclosed in torn cries, in embarrassed silences, in unconscious words.

In conclusion, dare I admit that in "The Tragedy of a Brain" I have sought to defend weakness, in the court of humanity, and to satirize the strong ("sensible people!") who demand bricks without straw from the weak.

SPECIAL NOTICE.

Owing to the nature of the plot, the author expressly repudiates any suggestion that the events or characters have any reference to persons living in the world of fact. It seems, therefore, advisable to disavow any intention of writing "*un roman a clef*"

BOOK I

AN ARABIAN NIGHT'S STORY

CHAPTER I

Nature and Art

My profession is the Law: I make no pretence to philanthropy, and I dislike sentiment. The good I may have done has not necessarily risen from the best motives. An idle and languid hour may have disposed me to watch hitherto unknown forces, and the play of strange motives, for mere amusement; and I may have found the sight of moral struggle and distress not altogether unpleasant. If then I feel it requisite to explain my interest in the following case, it is because I feel how far awakened sympathies tend to cloud the judgment.

My client entered my office by hazard, as he might have entered a shop; the only difference being that he was bold enough to hope to get a legal commodity without paying for it.

But before introducing my client I must explain how I come to be telling his story. I am not a writer of novels; nor, indeed, do I often read them. I have, however, read Cesar Birroteau (as a manual on Bankruptcy) and a few other works which are full either of charming technicalities or of naive ignorance of law. But writing that is a very different matter. I try to be accurate, clear, and brief; when I have a point, I know how to make it, but my words have more weight than fineness.

The author asked me, as an observer and a confidant in this affair, to co-operate with him in his work. I know, said I, only how to write documents. His reply to me was: That is precisely what I want you to do to draw up a document, *a human document.*

Case put that I consented; I asked him whether he would put my narrative into book-shape. To that he answered that he should therein exercise his discretion, which would probably teach him to let well alone.

But, I argued, a story in real life as we lawyers hear it, is so abrupt, full of natural gaps, suppressions, and possibilities which are latent.

Very well then, said he, leave Nature alone; I don't expect you to state things as they are, but as they seem. Abruptness is preferable to monotony; and as to suppressions, I find reticence charming—words can be used even by adventurers and fools, but Truth herself speaks in silences.

I pointed out that much of the story I had only noted in my client's own words the words of a mere boy, full of extravagances that suffering and anger had made him sometimes irrational, sometimes even silly.

He replied that he should not make a boy speak as a sage, that it was out of foolishness, weakness and the petty passions, that Nature drew her pathos.

He is an old friend, and I know that it is as futile arguing with his enthusiasm as with his despondency. At last I pretty strongly suggested that he would turn out such a book as had never been written, and that he was a fool for his pains. I will conclude by giving you his answer:

Let the man of letters be first of all a gentleman, and follow Thackeray. Grant it we are both fools, the great novelist has taught us not to obtrude that, or any other fact about ourselves, upon the Reader. Passions which have moved even you cry out for utterance: let such utterances find their own level, and let authors be the unseen instruments. You your dark office, tomes, deed-boxes, and dry sayings are only the frame of the picture: a suitable frame, plain, solid, and sombre. As to your style, it is that of the future, as the romantic and even the classic style will be a thing of the past. Witness our Master Stendhal, who cultivated the absence of rhetoric which is natural to you, and used to model his style on the Code Napoleon.

Naturalistic novelists (he, with some reason, continued) have lately taken the medical man and his laboratory for their models, a dissecting-room of dead matter and a profession notoriously materialistic; little wonder then if their works are lifeless. No; law and not medicine is the meeting-place of science and philosophy: the lawyer knows more of man-kind than the physiologist; and the deed-box contains more exclusively human interest than the medicine-chest. The "psychological moment" (as it is called) is to be studied in the cross-examination of witnesses, not in hospital clinics. Medicine has no place in works of combined imagination and observation; for if these deal with pathology, it is not that of the dissecting-rooms, but of law, custom, and institutions.

* * *

It was a very dull time that he came to me, some six years ago my strange client. I was thinking of shutting up the office, and going into the country for the week-end, when my clerk told me that a gentleman, who would not give his name, wished to see me. I ordered him to be shown in, suspecting from his refusing his name that he was someone who had got into "trouble" with the law, or perhaps a would-be borrower. But as I turned and looked at him, the formal words, "What can I do for you?" died on my lips, so frightened, strange, and questioning was his look. It was thus he spoke first

"Sir, I have no introduction to you, but I am in great distress, and I only ask you to give me a hearing. Afterwards you may see fit to help me, or you may not; but in any case it will relieve me to tell you my trouble."

I answered that I should be pleased to listen, and that he might safely tell me just as much as he thought fit; but that I would at once stop him if I found his communication likely to be of such a nature that I could not be privy to it.

With a curious mixture of impetuosity and embarrassment, he began a most extraordinary tale; and it is simply this tale which, with a few necessary comments, I now give to the reader, only premising that I have added in their place some details which he could not mention on his first visit.

CHAPTER II

"This man's metallic, at a sudden blow His soul rings hard."

I do not know where to begin. I think, however, I had better tell you what happened five months ago in the office of a money-lending solicitor, who does not enjoy a good reputation. I was within six months of coming of age, and I had just come up from Cambridge, where, like many other young men, I had made a fool of myself. In fact, I had spent a half-year's allowance in two months; and, pending my majority, my mother had agreed to make a weekly advance from my legacy, of which she was trustee. One day she told me to go to Mr. Winch, the solicitor, to receive this allowance— a strange proceeding, as that gentle man was not the family solicitor and was unknown to me.

On entering his room I saw two strangers sitting there. One was Mr. Winch, who wished me "Good day," and, after a peculiar pause, introduced his companion as "Mr. Wallace, an old and esteemed friend of your mother."

This stranger at once began in a ponderous tone to ask me a most astounding question: "Mr. Knollys, have you not an uncontrollable desire to take away your own life?"

Naturally I knew not what to say or do; I wondered if I was dreaming, or if my questioner was intoxicated. At last I stammered out "What an extraordinary question to ask a stranger. You cannot expect me to answer it"'

He continued, as if he had not even listened to my

reply, and as if he were hurrying through a tedious form, "Ah! And when you are in the street do you not think that people are going to kill you?"

I began to be alarmed, and to wonder, as I think anyone would, whether this man was out of his mind. I was moving to the door, when at the last look I recognised his face, and exclaimed, "Mr. Wallace, are you not really Dr. Walford?"

He changed colour, and asked whatever could put such an extraordinary idea into my head.

"My extraordinary idea," I replied, "was caused by your conduct, for an alienist is the only man privileged to ask such questions, and I recognise your face from a caricature. It was headed: 'How medical men advertise contrary to the etiquette of their profession' and hinted that you found in every notorious crime an opportunity for self-advertisement.'"

My indignation and the chance of turning the tables on him had carried me away, and it was only when I saw his face that I realised that I had made an enemy of the man who had me in his power. Without another word he left the room and signed a lunacy certificate.

Now, sir, I knew what the presence of Dr. Walford meant. I had had a dispute with my mother about money matters, and had threatened to appeal to the Court of Chancery, which would at least have halved her income. She said "Oh! We will see about that", and now was taking lunacy proceedings against me through a man whose very name was dreaded as a licensed rogue.

Danger brought me coolness and defiance. I saw that every word would be twisted and looked at from an alienist's standpoint, and that the greatest self-command would be needed to defeat them. I remembered that the law required two certificates, and was, therefore, not surprised when a newcomer entered.

He was about forty years of age, and his expression, though shrewd and collected, was not unkindly. "Ah! Mr. Knollys, I am a literary man, and your friends have asked me to get you placed on the staff of some good journal."

Looking him in the eyes, I replied "Sir, I have but this moment been interviewed by Dr. Walford with a view to proving me insane. Is it probable that 'my friends' would do this with a view to getting me employment on the press? Let me be frank: I know that you are a medical man doing your duty, and I will answer as calmly as I can whatever questions you may choose to ask me."

"Well, Mr. Knollys," he admitted, "we will not dispute the point. Allow me, then, to ask you if you have not a philosophical work for which you expect several thousand pounds?"

I protested that his was a leading question, but that I was not writing a book, and, if I were, should be glad to get a five-pound note for my first attempt.

"Well," he continued, "I suppose you get all your articles accepted."

This, of course, I denied, saying that I had indeed only sent some boyish essays to a parish magazine. Then he seriously began to ask me many questions on very different subjects, and, naturally, I took care to express none but the most moderate views, and even to make some allowance for his own personal equation. Thus when he opened a religious question, I remembered Sir T. Browne's *Tres medici duo atheistici,* and said, therefore, that within the boundaries of pure reason there was room for great difference of opinion, that what some men considered a matter for their conscience others deemed "a conventional lie of our civilisation," and cry, with Galileo, *il credere e cortesia,* and that anyhow religious heterodoxy was no longer a ground for imprisonment. When he next suggested that my affections were perverted, I firmly said that as long as I smarted under the injury of such an examination, I could not be expected to be unbiased, and that meanwhile calling the instigators my friends was simply begging the question.

Not the least interesting part was when he put the crucial question whether I was conscious of any eccentricity of character. I pointed out that I was at the *Sturm und Drang* period of life, the very time when slight eccentricities are natural, and even healthy signs of moral and mental growth, and added that what Balzac called his "congestion of ideas" was very different from brain disease.

"The world," I said at last, "places a fearful trust in your skill and honesty; your sentence, though it is secret and irresponsible, carries with it a life-long stigma, if not perpetual imprisonment. It is also final; for the negative is hard to prove, and one certificate of lunacy outweighs twenty of sanity. You know I am sane, you will not certify otherwise but more, I implore you, in my agony of dread, by all you hold sacred, to protect me."

Alas! His honesty was merely negative: he would not be mixed up in the affair, however sorry for me he might me. He left the room, saying that he could only promise me that he would have nothing to do with it, and immediately afterwards I heard him drive away.

* * *

My visitor's story was unexpected and even alarming. His demeanour, though agitated, showed no sign of mental disease; but so terrible is the stigma of such a charge, that I had from the first an uneasy feeling that there must be something in it. Nevertheless I determined to give him a fair hearing, and saying that he was telling his story with remarkable clearness, I asked him to continue.

CHAPTER III

The Jackal

"...slander,
Whose edge is sharper than the sword; whose tongue
Outvenoms all the worms of Nile; whose breath
Rides on the posting winds, and doth belie
All corners of the world."
                    Cymbelme.

I thought that, after all, their attempt against me would prove abortive, and my relief was intensified when Mr. Winch entered the room and proceeded to write a cheque for my allowance. When he had written it he left the room, with the explanation that he had to send it out to be cashed for me. I am not naturally suspicious, but the circumstances were so unusual, that I went to his cheque book and looked at the counterfoil, which should have been five pounds to Cecil Knollys, I found, however, that it was "£2 Self" which again aroused my apprehensions.

Then I went to the door and found it locked.

I heard a cab dash off, and I knew that they were trying to get another certificate; for, one step taken, they dared not stop.

What could I do, Sir? Many young men would say 'Why in the world did you stop there, why didn't you break the door down, get through the window, or cry for help? 'But had I done so, my violence would by my accusers have been construed into an indisputable symptom of madness. No, I could only wait and pray that such an utter rogue as Dr. Walford could not be found in London.

I had arrived all but punctual to my appointment at five: it was now past six. Thinking of all the terrible rumours of private asylums I began to be half-stupefied with dread. I sat a prisoner for what seemed many hours, but at eight o'clock the key was turned and Dr. Walford entered the room. He was arm in arm with an elderly man, and asked me, "Have you any objection to answering this gentleman a few questions?"To this I consented.

The new comer was very deaf. He took a chair very close to me, and said in a careless, husky tone, "Ah! Not been feeling very well lately. Been rather fast, billiards, and that sort of thing?"

I began to answer, "Well, I don't admit that, but I may have been foolish like many other youngsters on first going to a University, but that is all."

Scarcely had I uttered the words when he left the room, and I did not see him again. I naturally thought that seeing the common-sense way in which I had answered him, he had at once discovered that it was a case unworthy of consideration. However, the door was still locked, and in a few minutes a clerk came in and took from a shelf a small leather-bound book, which I at once saw was a Testament. Then I knew that all hope was lost, for they were about to swear to my lunacy.

I then went to the lawyer's desk, determined to write a note and send it to him. I was well aware that whatever I wrote might be misconstrued, so, although it cost me an effort, I wrote a merely formal letter, which I can repeat from memory.

18th December, 189— .

Sir,— This day I have been interviewed in your office by medical men, with a view to certify me a lunatic. I shall hold you responsible for whatever occurs here, and I demand, if I am judged insane, that I be sent to a public and not to a private asylum. You can have no *bona fide* reason for refusing this request.

After having knocked at the door till it was opened, I gave this letter to a clerk to deliver to Mr. Winch. As I did so I heard someone cry, "Lock that door!"

Lock that door!

CHAPTER IV

Descensus Averni

"Lasciate ogni speranzo a voi che'ntrate"
Inf. c. iii., 9.

Another half hour of awful suspense, another rattle of cabs in the street, and the door was once more opened.

"This way, sir," said the lawyer's clerk; and I saw two men standing in the passage. The one a man of perhaps fifty, the other some years younger— both, as I guessed, the keepers of some private asylum.

I needed all my courage not to break down. "One moment! Understand that I shall make no resistance, and you have no excuse for using any restraint." Then I followed the men to the door, and was hustled into a brougham and pair which was waiting.

Up the Strand we drove, past the Law Courts, through Leicester Square and the busy West End, leaving behind us the suburbs, and out into the open country. The one fellow sat by my side; the other, in front of me, almost pinioned my legs with his. At first not a word passed, but, on nearing the open fields, I asked where they were taking me. They replied that I must not excite myself, and that, as I was a little out of sorts, I was going to some friends in the country.

Then, trying to speak carelessly, I said, "I may be mad, but I am not a fool, and I know that I am on the way to an asylum. We left the lawyer's office at twenty minutes to nine, it is now nearly ten: when shall we get there? At least tell me where I am going."

The fellow made an evasive answer, and then, in order to make me lose my self- control, tried to frighten me by telling revolting tales of madhouses. He asked his friend whether he did not remember that nice young gentleman (just like this one, as reasonable as might be) whom they took to the same place. Poor fellow! He is chained to his cell now.

But even then I kept my temper, for I feared that if they put me under any physical restraint, I might actually lose my reason. The roads were becoming heavy and we went slowly. As a contrast to my misery, it was a resplendent moonlight night, and my attendants were in the best of spirits.

The horses came to a standstill outside a village inn, at a little past eleven, and here one of the men got out to ask the way, as I imagined, and to get some refreshment for himself. A small crowd soon gathered round the carriage, and now for the first time losing my presence of mind, I implored them to rescue me, saying that I was a sane man. But the moment the words escaped me I wished to draw them back, for the keeper gave a cool wink and touched his head, significantly, and the crowd of fools began to stare as if I were some wild beast show.

At last we continued our journey, which now seemed interminable. It was nearly one o'clock in the morning, and I was beginning to think that we had lost our way, when at last we drove through park gates to a House which stood hidden in trees some distance from the road. A bell was rung loudly, and a man, after a careful scrutiny, let us in, and I was gently pushed through a door which might have been inscribed with those words which the Florentine places over that of Avernus.

The proprietor was standing in the hall, and, leaving the attendants, I at once asked for a private interview on my reception.

"What! At this hour of the morning?" he exclaimed; but I retorted that if it were a proper time to bring me to such a place, it was a proper time to attend to me. "Very well then," he answered," what have you to say?"

"Doctor, I have been brought here as madman. I am not unwise enough to tell you that I am sane, because I know that every lunatic can say that. Anything I can say will not prove a negative. You can only discover my sanity by watching me carefully, and, in order that you may do so, I am prepared to stay here quietly, and to conform to reasonable regulations. All I beg you is to let the trial be a fair one, and not to place me amongst prejudicial surroundings."

He seemed surprised at such an address from a patient brought to his asylum in the middle of the night. "Well Sir" he said, "you have hit on a very ingenious way to prove your sanity: most lunatics, in fact, do tell us that they are sane. Be assured that you will be fairly treated here, and if it should prove that any mistake has been made in your case, you will undoubtedly be released"

"I naturally wonder how far you mean what you say. You will at least give a private room, and keep me apart from the other patients?"

The Doctor then rang a bell, and the night watchman appeared, was asked what private rooms were then disengaged, and named several. But now the Doctor looked at the letters which the attendants had brought from Dr. Walford, and his manner changed. He spoke rapidly and harshly, in obvious perplexity.

"I regret," he said simply," that we cannot accede to your request. "

He turned to the night watchman and told him to place me in room 11; and thus that very night, after eight hours' suspense, I found myself under lock and key in a room with lunatics.

* * *

My client paused, and I saw that he was thinking of scenes that were still full of horror for him. My doubts as to his sanity were disappearing, and I determined to let him tell me as much as he pleased without allowing him to go to useless or unnecessary pain in the recital. Before he continues I may mention that at this point I begin to supplement the narrative with a few details. It still, however, continues a narrative of plain and hideous fact: its full significance, the true character of mother and son, will appear later. And in this I follow Maupassant's dictum, *that Psychology should be concealed in the book, as it is in reality, under the facts existence.*

CHAPTER V

The Wandering Moon

The room is black darkness, but soon the moon casts a vague light between the shadows, showing the beds of unknown madness within reach of mine. Have you heard the moans of a sleeping dog, sir? Such were the sounds around me, and from a silent corner I almost fancied that I felt the influence of eyes lit with mania. How many tragedies are recorded in these sleepers of love, maybe, and ruin? Do they never dream of sanity, wake, and for a moment think and feel?

A dim shadow rises up in bed, mutters incoherent words—a foul expression and an oath, a sob, some woman's name and then sinks again into noiseless sleep.

Silence, memory, thought—these mute horrors around me, and the memories of the day and of the woman who loved me and was waiting.

In a corner someone rose suddenly. I heard the sound of bare feet as they furtively, slowly, came towards me. It was dark for the moment, but I knew that someone was standing by my bed, was bending over me. I heard his quick-drawn breath, and then I felt the thinness of a hand feeling my face as if in curiosity. In mortal dread I closed my eyes, and, as I felt the touch of a hand on my eyelid, there escaped me an echoing panic scream in which all the pent-up agony of a day was heard and told through every ward and den.

CHAPTER VI

A New Tribunal

It is morning. The madhouse bell wakes me from a swooning sleep, and for the first time I see the room and its occupants. But I have no time for reflections; it is time to be up—and suffering.

I will rapidly pass over the first days of my detention; the breakfast with the jibbering *vis a vis,* the neighbour a melancholiac, who had for ten years continually muttered "Dead and damned "; the blunted knives, a necessary precaution in a room with a hundred madmen; the Sunday prayers, in which the proprietor prayed for the fatherless and the captive whilst I pondered the *Exaudi Dens.*

My only hope now was that the asylum people might *bona fide* believe me to be mad, for in that case it might not be useless to prove my sanity. I piqued the curiosity of the keepers by making no complaint, and one of them soon told me that he had only to see my eye and step to know that I was sane. I soon learnt, however, that vulgarity and recklessness were considered the best proofs of sanity by men incapable of understanding much else.

When, after two days' suspense, the doctor asked me if I was feeling calmer, I suppressed my indignation, and quietly asked what were the grounds of my arrest.

He began the professional rigmarole by saying that I was suicidal. To which I answered that I had been a free man for nearly twenty-one years, during which my life had been in my own power, and that I had never made any attempt against it; that placing me in a hopeless place in such a morbid environment was not calculated to make me esteem life more. I added that he evidently knew the charge was absurd, since he was taking no precautions; that suicide could never be prevented whilst a window would furnish broken glass or a flight of stairs a broken neck.

"Dr. Walford," he then said, "asserts that, when you are in a street, you imagine that people are going to kill you."

"What," I cried! "Suicidal and fear people are going to kill me! Were I about to kill myself, I should not fear that anyone else would incur the terrible responsibility for me. The two charges are incompatible and, there fore, they at least come to nothing at all.

He then said that I was accused of thinking myself to be "Almighty God"—a phrase made more awful by the words he used.

I ventured to say that if he would tell me what he meant precisely by "Almighty God," I could then argue with him, but that otherwise the charge was sheer invention, and the blasphemy his.

Well, putting aside these eccentricities, which you deny, is it not true that you were about to marry a worthless woman?

I said that in my opinion this question did not pertain to his enquiry; but that, nevertheless, I would answer it if he would tell me to whom he referred.

He mentioned a certain name, admitting that the signer of certificates had confided that one of the real, though not ostensible, reasons for these proceedings was to prevent my ruining my life by an irrevocable step. Then lapsing into cant, which is easier than argument, he abused me for philandering with a married woman.

Sir, I cried, cannot you see how desperate all these charges are? What a picture you are conjuring up! A God who wants to kill himself, and is yet afraid of being killed in the street—a man who is about (on the eve of suicide) to incur an indissoluble marriage with a married woman.

Now, doctor, you are not much older than I am, but this place must speedily make you a man of the world. My so-called friends have bethought them that "if they throw enough mud, some of it must stick;" that though I may disprove each single charge, I cannot dispel the whole cloud of lies and show its origin in a fraudulent intent. They hope that people will wisely say there must be something in it all, there is no smoke without fire, there is a grain of truth in all the chaff. Thus they have not been content with exhibiting me as an ordinary prey to a single delusion, but they have made (what is as dangerous in such a case as a forensic double defence) a multiple attack, an indictment with alternative and contradictory counts.

I ask you, as a man of the world, can you not see the result? Why, man, they have overdone it!

CHAPTER VII

In the Nature of a Climax

My sleeping- room was on the first floor; the windows were locked. Each night I crept to them to pry them, and had hidden a long lavatory towel to form a rope. One night, it was about one o'clock; I found the window gave at my touch! I did not push it up for fear the cold air would wake the keeper. My clothes were outside the door, according to rule, and the sleeping keeper had the key. I crawled to his bed and, still on my knees, took the key from his pillow without waking him, unlocked the door, took my clothes, and dressed my boots last. Then I fastened my rope to the chair and pushed at the window. It only opened three inches. *It was half locked!* '

Quietly I undressed, replaced my clothes, locked myself in (only just before the watch-man passed), crawled to the keeper, and tremblingly gave back the key, and got into bed.

The next night I unscrewed a window and escaped. All night I walked, and in the morning found myself worn and overwrought at the door of the woman I loved. The very day I had been taken I should have carried her help and comfort in her illness and distress; I had disappeared in the hour of her need, and she had not heard of me for three months. But I forgot all my agony in my love; and when I knocked at her door, she sent a servant to say that she did not wish ever to see me again.

Then I understood what she had thought of me, and, going to a tavern, I wrote a letter, telling her all. I took this letter to her, but my hand was no sooner on her gate than I was lightly touched on the arm. It was the head keeper!

"I expect you did not think to see me here?"

"No; what then?"

"You are coming back, of course."

"You forget that you have no keepers or strong rooms here; we are man to man."

"Shut it. I have only to touch my head, and wink that you are mad, and every passer-by will hunt you down like a mad dog and you know it.

"Agreed! You can take advantage of the ignorant cowardice of the public, but so can I. I shall touch my head and say that *you* are mad. We shall be quits then.

"Oh no, we won't! I have *your certificates* and a witness. Now you have your choice; come freely, or come tied up, but come you must. Williams, take that letter from him."

* * *

They took me down by train. At the London Terminus (to save a scene) they did not stand within ten yards of me. There I walked, apparently a free man in the midst of my fellows, and yet was being dragged back to hopeless horrors by the mere force of a lunacy certificate in the pocket of a discharged groom.

* * *

Meanwhile my mother had heard with terror of my escape, and, through information obtained from stolen papers, had found Isabel's address, and had herself sent the keepers there in the hope that I should be taken back that same night by the last train. In fear for her own reputation she went to the station, and waited to see, lying hid in the waiting-room. I saw her there, and before the keepers could stop me, fawned at her feet, told her that she held my brain, my life, my very soul in her hands, for which, if there be any moral government of the world, she must account. And when tears and prayers were useless, and I saw her deliver me to the supreme agony of recapture, to madness, and, in the end, an awful death, I cursed her in her laughter, in her dreams, in her old age.

Sneers give way to fury, and, pretending not to know me, she said it was disgraceful that keepers should permit a madman to insult ladies; and I was carried away into the train.

CHAPTER VIII

The Question of the Soul

"...Eats into my sinews and dissolves my flesh to a pollution, poisoning the subtle, pure, and inmost spirit of life."
The Cenci.

My life after my return might form an epic of terror: no longer dazed with a sudden blow, I now fully realised my future, without reasonable hope. "You will not escape us again," was a mock I heard on every side.

Placed with forty patients in a gallery, which contained two doorless rooms and a padded cell, I was there confined from morning to night. Some were slowly dying from softening of the brain and became more helpless, filthier, day by day; some were epileptics, who had daily fits; the rest were raving madmen.

What sights and sounds! Shouts of blasphemy, obscenity, shrieks of despair; singing, sobbing, and—I hear it now—laughter. Fighting, beastliness, a frantic running—there was no respite for prayer, at meals, at any time. There was no holy semibreve of silence in this devil's anthem—this tarantella of sight and sound to which my thoughts danced into madness.

How could I sleep at night with sixteen others in a room which led to the dormitories of a hundred men? In these sights and sounds and fetid air, a young man, I never caught a glimpse of Nature undiseased. Between waking and sleeping I heard blasphemies which seemed to tell of a lost soul rather than a lost mind.

When at last I fell asleep, it was only to be dragged from the bed and placed in the day gallery. There, exhausted, I dosed day after day; and even in sleep, their cries, their touches mingled with my dreams. There was no oblivion.

At times the doctor came to look at me, but his visits his were "like those of angels, short and far between." He asked me if I was being cured of the delusion of sanity "time," he added, "works wonders."

He knew the power of tendency *plus* fear, *plus* environment; he calculated the contagion of numbers; he knew that every cry that pealed out into the night and broke my rest was the death-knell of my reason. Knowing this, I say, he was deliberately driving me mad for fear I should prove my sanity some day. Having succeeded, he would then juggle cause and effect, and justify his conduct by its result. It was my very brain he touched, but not my "person," and his conduct was legal.

CHAPTER IX

The Other Man

One evening as I was leaning at the locked door, which kept me from the convalescent and quieter cases, it was suddenly opened and a man was thrust in. He sat down and looked savagely round him, and for the moment I thought him a dangerous madman. But suddenly he seemed to pray, and in some way suspecting his sanity, I spoke to him.

"If you are a sane man, believe that I too may be sane, although we meet here. You have a friend, and God knows whether between us we may not both manage to escape."

He looked sullenly at me, but gave no answer. The next day, however, he asked my forgiveness for not responding to my kindness. He explained that he had found himself thrown amongst madmen by a trick, and knew not whom to trust.

The authorities soon saw that the alliance of two sane men was defeating their plans. It was hope which they saw in our eyes, which frightened them, and they separated us.

My friend, Herbert Lane, within a month made eight desperate attempts to escape. He had indomitable spirit, and though they bound him hand and foot, and threw him like a maniac into a padded room, he only renewed his attempt the next day. At last I heard that he was no longer in the asylum.

At the end of ten weeks from my recapture a keeper with whom I had tampered showed signs of giving way.

Shortly afterwards he was told to take a party of six "invalids" for exercise across the fields in the immediate neighbourhood. This was my opportunity.

I must here explain that, when I was recaptured, one of the keepers had offered, as a friend, to hide any papers or money for me, as I was about to be searched; but I at once guessed that it was a clever trick to obtain what I might otherwise have successfully concealed, and only gave him a few pence and some papers of little importance. I then wrapt a sovereign in some dirty paper, and threw it into a heap of rubbish which was permanently in one of the day rooms. This coin had never been discovered, and now, on hearing that I was to be taken out for exercise, I put it in my pocket.

Although it was a warm day, I took an ulster with me. I meant to escape and to die before I was recaptured. Here seemed my last hope of liberty and life: I must now "arise or be for ever fallen."

CHAPTER X

Libertatis sacra fames

"The man who makes his escape, we repeat, is inspired; the effort towards deliverance is no less surprising than the flight towards the sublime. The thirst for liberty changes intelligence into genius."
                                                    V. Hugo.

I knew that the keeper was irresolute, and feared lest he should betray me at the last moment. Therefore I did not tell him that I meant to escape, until we had reached a stile leading on to the high road which was the limit of our walk.

"Somers," I then said, "you have promised to help me to escape. Well, I only keep you to your promise: I shall run now, and if you attempt to catch me, you must leave these five who are lunatics. If you try and fail to catch me, you will still be blamed by your master, but you will get no help from me. On the other hand, delay notice of my escape for half an hour, and I will do what I can for you."

The man Somers was alarmed at his position, but carried away by my boldness and by the sight of the money which indicated friends outside, he exclaimed with an oath that escape I should. To deceive the cunning espionage of the lunatics, I shouted to him to go on whilst I tied a boot-lace; and when he had disappeared behind the hedge I ran.

Ran for life, ran with horror behind me, Life and Hope in front, and possible Vengeance in the distance.

After the first hundred yards I nearly fainted, so sudden and so terrible had been my effort. A moment I stopped, and then tore on—blood at the mouth. I overtook a trap, and feared that the driver would suspect and stop me. To avert suspicion, although I knew his horse could not go as fast as I, I asked him to give me a lift, as "I was running for a doctor."

I suppose he knew the truth, for he brusquely refused, saying that he was not going my way. However, as he made no attempt to catch me—it was a dangerous business, and not his—I soon left him far behind. Presently I neared a village, the streets all full of people coming out of church. I was still carrying my ulster (which I meant to sell), I was very flushed, and my tie was blooded. I cooled my face at a brook, turned my tie, and made myself walk slowly through the village, risking all on the chance that no telegram announcing my escape had yet arrived.

The village past, I ran again. Every sigh for freedom was repeated in each gasp for breath. Quicker! Quicker!! Quicker!!! Every moment I feared a trap must over take me. Before I reached the next town I knew the police would be warned by wire to be on the look out. I broke through a hedge to rest a moment, and then I saw something gleaming in the distance—the river! Could I but reach the other side, I might be safe.

I ran to the river bank. A pleasure party was passing, and I asked them to put me across, and they did so. The opposite tow-path reached, I felt safe. I plunged into some fields out of sight of the river, and, hidden under a hedge, I fainted.

When I revived it was sunset and was getting cold; but before night I wished to run to earth in the great city. I saw the bridge in the distance, and walked rapidly on; but before reaching there, I deliberated.

I dare not go to the railway station, as they would have

wired my description down the line, nor dare I walk along the road for fear of the police or a trap from the asylum. The only other way was to follow the winding tow-path, and by this I could not reach London that night.

But when I reached the bridge I throbbed with happiness at the sight of a mob of excursionists, pleasure 'busses, and 9d. tea-houses. I entered one of these, for I knew that no one would think of looking for me there, and the good woman was too busy to scrutinise her customers. Having rested a little, I thought boldness shall carry me through, and, hidden in a crowd of merrymakers, I rode to London on the top of a four-in-hand omnibus.

BOOK II

THE CYNIC

CHAPTER I

A Study in Irrelevance

*"The first chapter of every book was not to continue the nar-
rative, but should consist of anything the author chose to
entertain his reader with."*
On the New Species of Writing (1730).

Our old-fashioned novelists knew how to tell a story,
and did not break into it with unseemly controversies
or explanations. All digressive matter they relegated to
a special chapter, which was avowedly irrelevant, whilst
they reserved the rest of the book for story-telling and
nothing else. No author can tell a good story if he continually interrupts it with little speeches to the reader:
the old style seems much better—to wait like a decent
theatrical manager to address the house between the
acts.

In this experimental chapter, the author seeks to place
the reader at his own point of view, and to explain why
he has reduced the second book to about one tenth of
its prosaic proportions.

The course of the story now takes us to the examination of evidence, the detection of motives, and other
business-like subjects, which, however admirable in
detective stories, seem out of place in a novel. Without
self- restraint and careful reticence, indeed, the work of
imagination will slip into the Blue Book spirit.

A man of genius paradoxically said that it is a great
pity for a literary artist to have a story, as he would probably tell it. If the mere enumeration of sordid crimes and

common-place motives would weaken my story, and if I can heighten its effect by a bold neglect of such details, what matter if the Gradgrinds of fiction condemn it as "inadequate?"

Eclaircissement is so often inartistic.

CHAPTER II

The Narrative Continues

My client was now nearing the end of his long story, and worn with the fatigue and excitement, spoke briefly and rapidly. In this way he gave me but a faint idea of the fantastic adventures of a hunted man in London. Such adventures might fill many a chapter with interest and sensation, but the facts are almost too bizarre for serious fiction, and are not essential to the story. What follows, therefore, is merely a hurried summary of his concluding words.

On reaching London, he took his conspicuous overcoat to a railway cloak room, and then went to a cheap lodging-house. There he met an artist named Halifax, a scapegrace indeed, but yet a kindly gentleman. Cecil confided in him, and they began, by his advice, a strange search for some unlikely hiding-place. They had first gone to a Roman Catholic "Home for the Dying," to which the artist had subscribed through all his straits. But here the matron, though an old friend, was obliged to refuse Cecil a refuge, but suggested another. This turned out to be a house which boldly announced from every window that it was a "Governess Agency and Home." It was now deserted, however, and the rooms were to let. Halifax satisfied the landlady in some ingenious way as to his companion's lack of baggage, gave the address of some relative by way of reference, and took the rooms. He then remembered that an old medical friend was living near, and him he asked to visit Cecil, and, with his consent, to report on his mental condition. After a week of inaction, Cecil took the matter into his own hands, and, having seen my name reported in some small case, was come to me.

His Arabian Night-like story had set my brain in a whirl. I was surprised to find it eight o'clock, and the city streets all deserted. But, however late it might be, I was deter mined to have some proof of his account that very night. Not that I believed it, for I am not of a credulous disposition, but the story was so connected, and had, moreover, so surprised my interest, that some examination of it seemed imperative.

Hitherto I had been afraid to question him lest I should embarrass the flow of his narrative, but I now asked him for definite names and addresses.

"Here," he replied, "is the certificate and address of Dr. Friendly, also that of my friend Mr. Halifax, and of my private tutor, who knew me before these events. This is the name of the asylum in which I was confined, and whose servants are at present searching for me."

"You see that I have given you my whole confidence. Now for the first step which I beg you to take. Will you write to the asylum and enquire whether I was confined there, and ask for a copy of the certificates? You can then compare them with what you yourself see, and with all the evidence I may be able to bring you as to my sanity. Why! I can bring witnesses— both those who knew me up to the very day when I was captured, and those who have known me since the day I escaped."

Then, when I had noted the addresses in my pocket-book, he left me. I had been on the point of asking my strange client to come with me to my house, but second thoughts cautioned me against committing myself, as yet, in any way. So I merely promised to make some enquiries, and asked him to call on the following Thursday.

CHAPTER III

First Steps

That same night I took the first steps in the elucidation of this curious case. I am tempted to continue the story by simply giving a copy of the subsequent correspondence; but it is not the most interesting form of narration, and brings in much that might well be omitted. I wrote first to Mr. Halifax and Dr. Friendly, and asked them to call on me, and then I sent the following carefully considered letter to the Asylum proprietors:

MONUMENT CHAMBERS, E.G. 3 July, 189—.

W. FRANCIS, Esq., M.D., F.R.C.S.

Dear Sir,—Mr. Cecil Knollys has consulted me, and states that he escaped from your house on the 15th instant, having been there confined for five months.

He alleges that he was a sane man when you received him, and this statement seems to be supported by his present language and conduct. He declares his certificates to have been signed by Walford, who is well known, and by a Dr. Harding, who has since become bankrupt and left his hospital.

I am now applying to you for a copy of these certificates; but I may add that I am not at present an advocate of Mr. Sackville's case, and shall be ready to consider any contradiction of his statements which you may see fit to send me. Is it true that he has been confined in a passage with forty dangerous lunatics during the day, and placed to sleep with sixteen noisy cases?

I am, &c.,

J.G.

I posted the letter myself, and, on my return, sat down to consider Dr. Friendly's certificate, which ran as follows:

I have to certify that I have had Mr. Cecil Knollys under my constant and earnest observation for the last week. I have had long conversations with him on tentative subjects, have received letters from him, and have admitted him to my family circle. His state of mind is incompatible with any form of mania which I have ever seen. Indeed, it is at present not too much to say that he is an epitome of absolute sanity. I have, therefore, come to the conclusion that any allegation of recent mental disease is utterly out of the question, and this opinion I shall be prepared to support if occasion arises.

(Signed) HORACE FRIENDLY, M.D., F.R.C.S.

Now how far can I rely on this certificate of sanity? Is Dr. Friendly sufficiently skilled in this department of his profession? Is it indeed certain that he has ever even seen a lunatic, or has received the most rudimentary instruction in psychological medicine? Is even a week time enough to form an opinion of any value? Is he himself of good character, prudent, and unprejudiced? But why need I ask these questions, when the law of this country asks none before allowing the same man to certify lunacy, practically beyond the possibility of contradiction?

CHAPTER IV

A Friend

I was in the midst of my morning correspondence, the following Thursday, when my clerk announced Mr. Halifax. I thanked him for his visit and then asked him to tell me whatever he knew about Mr. Knollys' story. I found his account to be substantially the same as that already given by Mr. Knollys himself. To this, however, he added the following comments.

"Mr. Knollys," he said, "had shown no signs of aberration, although naturally he showed great mental distress. This, however, he had at first attributed to some love-tale; and, Knollys, indeed, in order to elude the curiosity of some bystanders, had once audibly muttered some such phrases as 'Curse the girl' and talked of enlistment."

As to the details of the young man's account, he was disposed to believe it not much exaggerated, but he acknowledged that his artistic temperament was prejudiced in favour of the unusual. That the man was sane was evident enough, and to his mind had always been so. If, therefore, the proprietor admitted the detention of such a man for so many months, his report of his treatment during that time must be largely discredited.

At this point I suggested that Mr. Halifax might like to give me some information about himself. He very sensibly took my hint, and explained that, owing to what he called "a Bohemian aversion to inhabited house duty," he lived for the most part at an inn, in a garret, or even at some small lodging-house; but that he retained his studio and sanctum in the house of his mother, the Hon. Mrs. Halifax.

When I asked him what he knew about Dr. Friendly, his answer was simple but conclusive. He said that, appreciating Knollys' great need and wishing to be helpful to him, he had thought over all his acquaintance in search of an honest and kindly man, who would advise him in a disinterested manner.

After this charming tribute to his friend's character, Mr. Halifax left me, after asking me to do my utmost in the cause of misfortune.

CHAPTER V

The Other Side

The reply which I had that morning received from the asylum was much as I expected. Of course they denied the accuracy and truthfulness of my client; but they delayed sending copies of certificates under the pretext of a claim for fee. This to me seemed proof enough that they were actually signed by Messrs. Walford and Harding; for, if not, Dr. Francis would have discredited my client's charges by proving the certificates to be otherwise signed. It is always easy for a brazen witness to deny a whole story; but in this case he does not adduce any one fact as false.

The idea struck me at this moment that I must have recently seen the name of Dr. Harding somewhere; and after a short search my clerk brought me a week-old report of his bankruptcy, which had been somewhat notorious. In his public examination it appeared that he had been for some time insolvent, and, knowing himself to be so, he had lightly incurred heavy liabilities in regard to a certain charitable undertaking (probably with no worse intention than self advertisement).

By a comparison of dates, it proved, that on the day on which after three minutes' examination he had consigned my client to a madhouse by his certificate, his signature for twenty shillings would not have been honoured by any bank or other business concern in London.

As to the other signatory, Dr. Walford, he was a gentleman whose name was quite familiar to me, and I had occasionally seen him in the Law Courts.

CHAPTER VI

When Doctors Disagree

"And here, I take it, is the doctor come," I might have quoted, as my clerk announced another visitor. "Pray be seated: and accept my thanks for coming."

Hardly had I uttered the words, when I recognised in Dr. Friendly an old college acquaintance. From the little I remembered of him, I knew him to be an honest and able man, whose excessive modesty alone had kept him from advancement. I at once recalled myself to his recollection, and he spoke without constraint.

"Well, Griffiths, this appears to be a most extraordinary case, and as the man has by some chance, or may be Providence, hit on you from amongst thousands of London lawyers, you will feel it a duty to investigate the case in a kindly manner, I am sure."

"My own feelings entirely. We lawyers, however, must not be talked over by the first clever tongue; that would be turning the tables indeed."

"Still, the man's story must be true, or he has an imagination which has mistaken its vocation"

"His story has in great part been negatively proved by a letter I have just received from the asylum, which you shall see. But you, yourself, tell me candidly, do you consider him perfectly normal?"

At this he laughed. "Abnormal," he replied, "sounds a dreadful accusation, but what does it mean? Why it only means, as Dr Johnson would have said, 'above or below mediocrity.' It is the favourite word of mediocrities!"

"An expert," he went on to say, "is a most unreliable authority in lunacy matters. There is, at present, no system of instruction in mental pathology, and its *soi disant* professors supply the want of exact knowledge by a little bluster and most extravagant assumptions. ' There is no system of instruction in psychological medicine,' says one eminent physician, 'because there is no definite knowledge to be imparted'"'

"In this indefinite state of the science, you may, by making names mean what you will, suppress all individuality. If, in the last resort, the sanity of your subject seems impregnable, you may then prove him mad because he is sane. This is no exaggeration, for I myself once saw what was called *'want of the physiological unreason proper to the age'* given as a proof of lunacy by a so- called expert! "

But I am being carried away from our story. After some further conversation, my friend, after a cordial invitation to his rooms, left me; and I then continued my investigations in another direction.

CHAPTER VII

Searching the Registers

Before seeing Mr. Knollys I was anxious to test certain statements as to his position, by consulting the Registry of Wills at Somerset House.

On my way I passed the scene of the alleged drama, which was one of the many streets leading off the Strand. I dismissed my cab and sauntered down this street, which is very secluded, but which was probably all abuzz at the present moment in consequence of my letter. In passing I recognised the money-lender's house, and when I returned, after walking a few steps further, I saw Dr. Walford hurriedly leaving the office. This, then, proved another fact in issue, the connection of the usurer with these proceedings in lunacy.

Now for Somerset House. My client claims under the Will of his aunt, Miss Agnes Knollys, to be entitled to a legacy of £2,000, of which his mother is trustee.

At the Registry I asked for the book KN— but it was already engaged. Shortly afterwards it was handed to me by the user Dr. Walford! I opened the book at hazard, and at once found the Will of Miss Agnes Knollys, of Winstead, Sussex.

"To my dear nephew, Cecil Knollys, I bequeath the sum of ##2000 to be held in trust by Mr. N., Solicitor." Further on, however, I found a provision which empowered the executors to pay the fund over to Mrs. Knollys (the mother), whose receipt should be a full discharge.

On this point I consider the proof to be ample. My next step, then, is to investigate Mr. Winch's professional reputation. He is alleged to be a money-lender, and as I am at Somerset House, I will look over the Bills of Sale. On enquiry, however, I found that these Registers were now kept at the Law Courts to which I proceeded. My intention was to look over all the Bills of Sale held by Winch, but I found that this obvious mode of tracing dubious transactions was impossible in the absence of an index of holders. I was obliged, therefore, to be guided by my suspicions, and first enquired whether Dr. Francis himself had given any such security, but was unable to trace one. Then I remembered Thomas's bankruptcy, and looking under his name, found, as I half expected, that he had given a Bill of Sale to Mr. Winch, and was in his power, therefore, when in his office he signed a certificate of lunacy. His certificate protects the proprietor; the proprietor protects the relative: it is a mutual indemnity association, and there is no risk.

CHAPTER VIII

A Startling Incident

As I returned, my mind reverted to the almost forgotten tale of Valentine Vox and to those of Charles Reade, who used to boast that he knew the lunacy trade *"intus et in cute"* My mind conjured up the memory of that scene, read years ago, of a lunacy trial, "the court full of the low faces of keepers, all ready to swear him mad" and can it have been overwrought fancy when I looked up I saw two such faces watching the entrance to my office from the other side of the road.

It was no fancy. In writing to the asylum, I had naturally given my address, and they were now watching my office to catch my client. Suddenly I remembered that Cecil Knollys had an appointment with me for that very hour. What was to be done? It was futile to talk of giving the scoundrels in charge; for they had the law on their side, and had I my office filled with all the experts in London, ready to swear to my client's sanity, these keepers could still have carried him off before our very eyes.

The thought of such an indignity put me on my mettle: I walked quietly to the entrance, but once out of sight I raced up the stairs and shouted to my clerk to get his hat. I told him to go to the one end of the street and to wait for Mr. Knollys, to tell him of his danger, and take him in a cab to London Bridge Railway Station. I myself then rushed downstairs, passed the two men, and, turning the corner, took up my position at the other end of the street

I was afraid to leave my post, and therefore waited an hour before I went back to the office. My clerk had not returned, and, on going to his end of the street, I found him gone. On driving to the station I found him in a waiting room with my client, who was in great excitement at his narrow escape. This he now told me was not the first attempt that had been made against him.

Only the day before he had been horrified to see a keeper in the distance, who had just caught sight of him. Instinctively looking round for any means of defence or flight, he was fortunate enough to see a constable. The keepers seeing their quarry at a standstill, slackened their pace, but it was still a race of seconds. A cab was standing at the curb, and well—Necessity is the mother of invention.

"Constable," he said steadily, "I have just come from withdrawing some money from the bank, and I notice that I have been followed ever since by two men."

"Oh, well! You leave them to me, sir," was the complacent reply. "You just jump into a cab. Here coachmen," he cried, "look smart, the gentleman is in a hurry."

I was no sooner on the step but the keepers rushed up, and tried to catch at the cab. The constable, however, pulled them back, at the same time calling put sharply, "All right, cabman, you drive off."

The horse sprang off, jerking me back wards, but as I fell in a heap in the cab I just caught sight of my pursuers being arrested as suspicious characters. Before the explanations could be made much to the chagrin of my unconscious protector—I was safe.

CHAPTER IX

An Invitation

One thing was clear: my client could not afford to run such risks; and it was evident enough that the anxiety was already preying on his mind. His fear was so overwhelming, that he began to look with suspicion even on me, and his eyes seemed to ask me if my sympathy was growing cold or tired.

I, therefore, expressed myself in terms which I have since seen reason to deem precipitate, and asked him to go into the country with me.

He first objected, honestly enough, on the plea of expense, but at last consented. "It's not the pleasant country which tempts me to accept your offer," he said, "though that is cheery and undiseased and a solace to eyes still aching with prison walls, but it is a refuge for the hunted man, where there will be no new faces to scan and dread."

Accordingly, we went down to the country together, and there he told me an incident of his past life— "a sea voyage for health"—which may not have been without significance, both as furnishing precedent and thus also, in part, motive for the mother's conduct. To preserve to my narrative a fitting length, which is a "unity" too much neglected, I have omitted this story here, reserving for after consideration the expediency of adding it at the end of the book as a fitting "Appendix " to a novel—a short story. If space forbids this, I need only say that, in the course of a disgraceful scheme of neglect in his youth, the mother had sent a compromising letter, which had passed into the son's hands, and had now been seized by her.

CHAPTER X

Mother and Son

The certificates were not yet expired, when I received a letter from my client's mother, asking to be allowed to call on me. The position of affairs was most unsatisfactory, the excitement preying on my client's mind, so that I was very anxious to bring about, if not a reconciliation, at least some kind of *modus vivendi*. At present, too, he was virtually dependent on me, and I had many other claims upon me.

I therefore wrote to the mother, thanking her for her letter, and suggested that if she would meet me at a place named, I might be able, should she wish it, to bring about a meeting with her son, with a view to compromise. To this she replied, by wire, that she would be at the place indicated in my letter by five o'clock that same day.

My client, when I called at his rooms, was out, and I was surprised to hear from the servant that probably he was walking in the neighbouring cemetery. I soon, however, guessed that he had considered this to be an uncommonly good hiding-place, owing to its being unpatrolled by the police.

The mother was not far off, so I decided to fetch her, hoping that the solemnity of the place of meeting might restrain unseemly passions. It was not without reluctance that she accompanied me, and when we found the son standing by a tomb, she bitterly demanded "what this posing meant."

The answer betrayed the weakness of my client's character. Making all allowance for his excitement, it was unseemly and melodramatic; and to my mind evinced a certain underlying insincerity.

"My poor father rests here," he said. "I am taking refuge from a mother's cruelty at a father's grave."

The mother recoiled, and I was much shocked, and told him how wrong it was to speak to his mother like that that he must now try to bury the past.

"You've betrayed my confidence," he cried, "in seeing my mother at all, and in bringing her here. Don't prate to me about burying the past. I am a son of hate, and one past, a horrible marriage lies buried here. But my past—it is myself: my life, my brain that you can't bury till you bury me."

I must say I lost patience: here am I doing my utmost for him, and he turns and accuses me of breach of confidence. I should have thrown up the case in despair, had not the mother acted most unexpectedly.

"You are wrong," she cried, "quite wrong. Whatever I have done, I have done with the best intentions. I am speaking for your own sake what good can you do by fighting against me? Even if you could reduce my income by throwing our affairs into Chancery, you would be penniless. Will you tell all the world that you have been in a madhouse? Who would credit your story? Believe me; you would harm yourself much more than me. Be wise; return to the University, and say nothing to brand you with an ineradicable stigma."

She argued, appealed, threatened. She almost convinced me that she had not been a free agent; and her cleverness and tact made one pass over self-contra-dictions.

Nevertheless I did not lose sight of the obviously venal motives for her change of front. I inwardly summed up the matter in the cynical quotation "that seeing the exceeding difficulty of putting salt on the bird's tail, she considered the advisability of throwing dust in the bird's eyes." This notwithstanding, seeing no other course open, I urged him to consent to an arrangement which would secure him the means of continuing his studies, myself undertaking to guard him from any further proceedings in lunacy.

Such, as far as I am concerned, was the end of this story of strange adventures, and undisclosed intrigue. I have only to add a few remarks on the immediate sequel.

CHAPTER XI

Failure?

"Le secret d'ennuyer est de tout dire"

I am sorry to say that Cecil Knollys turned out a failure, a man utterly impractical. This impracticability, joined to certain innuendoes of the mother (whom I now saw occasionally), led me to doubt his perfect sanity. At last I was boldly told that certain papers existed which were conclusive proof of his insanity. I only hint at this mystery, and give the answer of the son when I had a short opportunity to ask him for an explanation. He said that by interleaving a fragmentary diary, scattered psychological notes, and a sensational story, you might make a whole incomprehensible enough. He defied me to give any credit to papers disavowed, obtained by stealth, and, for all he knew, supplemented by forgery.

When taxed with lack of resolution, he said "My will to will may be passionately strong, but my will itself be weak."

Such a quibbling reply was far from satisfactory to me, and as he seemed no longer to be in danger, I tacitly closed the acquaintance with an irritating sense of disappointment.

BOOK III

THE TRAGEDY OF A BRAIN

CHAPTER I

"Comprendre c'est pardonner"

While discussing the importance of happy or unhappy "endings " of novels, we seem to forget that interesting and significant lives of men and women do not run on the lines of a "plot," and that mechanical endings are Sacrifices to a mere convention. Nature, indeed, may have its melodramatic moments; but marriage despair, and other current catastrophes, so far from being "endings," are but prologues to a great and more human play.

This is the drama of character, which is enacted within, the sealed doors of the mind. Real documents and reportable intrigue seem here as banal as the realistic effects of the "transpontine" stage. Some catastrophe has occurred, the instinct of self-preservation has been violently aroused, and the outer life then becomes uneventful. But look within, and we shall see this manly instinct becoming, in silence and solitude, a mere brutish selfishness, or we find a heart broken by heartlessness deadening itself in recklessness and gross appetite. Still at times we find a far nobler drama.

Is there, then, no hope for any clear and vivid sketch, some articulate cry, from these unseen tragedies whose existence we feel at times when we look into each other's eyes? Will no "misunderstood" man deign thus to defend himself?

Such a defence let me attempt.

* * *

Some months after the foregoing events, I, Cecil's friend, met Mr. Griffiths, the lawyer, in the Strand.

He then told me that Cecil was "a failure," and that he should probably see no more of him. He declared that he was lethargic, unambitious, and of a very unamiable temper; that, though he worked "by fits and starts" in a most unpractical way, he accomplished nothing. He said that he wished to make every allowance (but made none) that it was very sad to see a young man—

Here I interrupted him impatiently, for I, on the other hand, thought that it was Griffiths who had failed—failed to see that Cecil was coming through a long convalescence of terror and suspicion and that he was now (to use Coleridge's simile) "telling a man paralysed in both arms to cure himself by rubbing them briskly together." The lawyer having thus left the tale a fragment, I, the friend who best understood him, may fitly finish it, not impartially, perhaps, but with something of hope and kindliness.

Having written to ask Cecil to come and see me, I received a short note to say that he could not come, as he was sailing from Liverpool the next day. I went at once to his rooms, where I found him in all the disorder of packing; and then I, his alter ego, with difficulty drew from him the statement which will follow.

This at last he allowed me to repeat. He adjured me, if his story must be told, to banish from it the lawyer's self-restraint, and not to tell it as the lawyer knew it. "Tell my story," he cried, "as I know it; let my despair speak close to some reader's heart."

And then he revealed to me a state of mind which I shall never forget; for, when he spoke of arrested growth and the racked soul, it seemed to me that weakness itself was pleading at the bar of humanity, from out the Inferno which may dwell in a man's own brain.

CHAPTER II

The House of Art

"Show me the man's Library, and I will tell you what he is."
Unverified Quotation.

When I arrived, I was shewn into his room, and was told he would return in a few minutes. His room, as I said, was in all the disorder of packing, but, whilst his other belongings were lying in utter confusion, his books remained in order in their places. And so, before I received the confidence that he was about to give me, I had an involuntary revelation of the man's character as stamped on his surroundings *chez soi*. I will not refer to the indications of recklessness and want of method, which were no more than I expected; but it was turning to his books that I came to the man in a new light. His single room at a few shillings a week then seemed to disappear, and what a strange edifice of thought and feeling did I then divine in looking at those orderly book shelves.

The stabile foundations of Kant's "absolute" philosophy, a chapel vibrating with the grand organ note of Milton, and (instead of the sordid tenement) here rises a glorious studio holding the elegance of Pater, the colour of Flaubert, the jewelled wordery of Gautier, and the music of Mallarme. From a corner peer out the Wiertz-like images of Poe and Hawthorne. Lighter reading too, of long ago, whispered of love from the *libri amoris* of Bullen and Garnett, but these, with the pleasant foliage of Peacock, were now covered with dust. From the books instead seemed to step out, to people the room and sympathise together, the victims of evil parentage

Richard Savage, Beatrice Cenci, and (on the other hand) the no less real figure of Papa Goriot.

Not to weary the reader, I have not continued the metaphor; but works yet more serious and dread were there works on brain disease, in which he would look, fearing that they should turn, as it were, to mirrors. But, in short, he had sought to rebut the charge of mental balance by profound studies which, whilst they left him few mysteries to shelter latent "mysticism" may, perchance have left him sadly disillusioned. I turned from the books, sadly, thinking that though they constituted against baseness and delusion an all but impregnable fortress, and a considerable barrier against error, that nevertheless no fortress could keep out mental pest or famine of the heart. In the face, however, of such evidence, what but stupidity could believe him a *vaurien*, or a do-nothing?

And now Cecil returned, alert, and labouring under the excitement of some momentous resolution. I asked him what his plans were, and urged him to do nothing rash. He turned on me then, "When I do nothing," he cried, "I am accused of 'doubting madness.' When I seek help or advice, I am told that I must live my own life. When I act for myself, I am told 'to do nothing rash.' Because I am a wronged man, everyone presumes to dictate to me and judge me. You are my best, my true friend: forgive my temper, I have just been to say goodbye to the lawyer, and even he has thrown 'failure' in my teeth."

I tried to argue with him, but every word showed me how futile it was for me to talk down such a case as his. What he told me, I repeat in his own words: what I said was pathetically futile, and I have suppressed it. I have not sought to turn his passion into a connected narrative. I believe it will appeal best as it is to those who are capable of understanding it. The imagination of such a reader will, I think, be able to supply a connection to the passages. The statement is purposely much curtailed for the duration of excitement is limited by a psychic law. To break up so brief a statement into chapters is not usual, but such divisions represent actual breaks in the thought or emotional pauses. The poetical headings, too, may serve as signal-lights to warn away unsympathetic readers.

CHAPTER III

Bricks Without Straw

"Who accuses me, and of what?"

Those who arrest my body—no! Arrest my growth, fill my consciousness with horror, and steal my very soul. Do they then judge me? Blame the racked body for its twisted limbs, the tortured soul for its deformity. Then exhort me to make bricks without straw, resolutions without brain tissue. Demand responsibility from a vegetable life, courage from a broken spirit, affection from nature disnatured by unnatural wrong. Seek smiles from what may be the death-bed of sanity, and, when you have got them, call them insincere.

CHAPTER IV

Long Ago

"My body independent as my soul."
Savage.

I to disappoint hopes! I, whose hopes were murdered? Only a year ago I was a mere boy, no less solitary, may be, than now, but then beauty, not horror, was within. All alone, I wandered into the world of mind, of books. Launched upon life without an oar, it was as if some benignant current had taken me to the islands of the blessed. Scarcely had I read one book (it was Marius the Epicurean), but it gave me my bearings; I turned on a full tide of feeling, and ran before the wind of thought, from what I was to what I might be. The great writers marked my course, like stars, to which I turned in solemn reverence. My ambition was pure; I loved. My consciousness was full of beauty and the dreams of night were filled with faces which expressed not individuals but passions of love, to me, true angels of Heaven.

The while I was living with the poet A. de Musset, the analyst Beyle, the philosopher Kant, preserving a "literary conscience," looking forward to many years of initiate virgin of petty success, I was looked on as idle, ignorant, and worthless. Still it was nothing to me. I lived with "the real people of the human comedy" not with the shadows around me, who hurried to and fro for the sake of boasting that they did so. I had to contend with baseness, but I took it into my world of thought, and it became, "point de serpent, ni de monstre odieux. Qui par l'art imité ne puisse plaire aux yeux"

My surroundings were base, my life lonely and yearning, but sleep filled with the pure and tender aspirations of the day sleep was a self-made home, and filled with gentle comfort.

Far away now is that quest of the Holy Grail of a better self. "My sun is gone down in the day time"; and, if the brain indeed be heaven or hell, my heaven is taken, and the brain filled with fire.

For now the faces I see, when I cower hiding, panting in a dream of capture, are the faces of mothers who lie in wait and mutter, "There he is!" Her voice, her face, horribly transfigured, linger on my senses when I awake. Only dreams! Dreams of a few seconds, but in one night of "circling" minutes a planetary of fear.

CHAPTER V

The Tragic Stage

"Eyes, filled with perishing dreams, and with wrecks of forgotten delirium."
Our Lady of Sighs.

The tragic stage of memory has other acts—scenes of love, destitute sickness, and domestic hate.

The chapter of love: that is a short story, but a tragedy in little. The sordid room (on the ground floor so near the heedless passers by), the woman, pallid with "the white heat of passion," anaemic, fanciful, and weak, living in a literature of noble imagination, intoxicated with self-sacrifice, acts—acts the part of baseness to the man she would save, because, woman-like, with attenoe au coeur au cerveau, she trembled with a premonition of approaching sorrow.

Can I forget how sick and destitute I lay in fever in a noisome shelter, and lest I should betray myself in delirious sleep, dragged my way out along the streets and bridges? To sleep! To be harried by dreams of capture and flight through all the terrible houses and highways of sleep. Half awake, to be dimly conscious of fighting among these terrors to hold back madness until dawn.

And then the home. Habit soon tells when the process of digestion makes the most irritation possible, the precise time to offer food when the body is too faint to receive it, and a concession when the heart is too indignant to accept. Until at last one goes out with a tetanus in every nerve, and would rather pluck bread from the fingers of the plague than return. Such are the fights of which only the exhaustion is seen.

CHAPTER VI

Moral Tactics

When a military leader has but few troops, and they disorganised, undrilled, and discouraged by the authorities at home, yet fights on and dies fighting, has he failed? Take a town besieged: the protectors worn out by being ever on guard, the town naturally weak and unfortified. A strong force besieges, and yet the commander not only refuses to surrender, but even rallying by glorious sallies throws back the besiegers from the town. He knows that in time the town must be taken: it can only be a matter of days; and yet in the name of honour alone he holds out to the death.

And so do I, with few inherited virtues, no instruction in principles, energies disorganised by watchfulness, terror and failure. Shall I then, having received the royal commission of life, but being unequipped for the struggle, return the commission life to the Giver rather than do ill? No; that is a felony upon myself.

I speak to softer sternness not for myself; for my old self is dying tomorrow. But I feel that a more skilful umpire than the world will see the heroism of weakness, the glory of reluctant ignominy, and the paramount claim of the weak, the forsaken, and the loveless.

CHAPTER VII

New Life

"Magic casements, opening on the foam of perilous seas, in faery lands forlorn."
Keats.

I am going to begin a new life. I was never told what a principle meant, and tried good and evil first one and then the other as a stranger to them must do. No course had been marked out to me, my eye had been directed to no centre, and yet I was blamed for eccentricity. I must begin as if I were a child. I shall put myself to a good school—the army. Then, with acquired habits of duty and discipline, with the character earned in the army, otherwise without a past or name, I shall set out to make, not my fortune, but my life, make my home, find love and kindred—in a novel sense a self-made man.

CONCLUSION

"I wonder whether he did repent ... The probability is, he fancied that his son had injured him very much and forgave him on his death-bed"
Round About Papers (De Finibus]

Conclusion—nay, art never concludes, and poetic justice is within.

When the furies, growing bold, crept from her brain and overspread her face, when her voice made men ponder the mystery of evil, when no longer could she "smile and smile and be a villain"—did the mother go mad? She is his mother; eternity only serves to bring them together, for ever and ever mother and son. Bound by no Church or Law, but bound by flesh and blood and spirit; between them is no divorce.

Will he then come back, and, in the calmness of strength, having received success as a pledge of hope, seek with strong nerve and faith and fundamental love to win her, his happy ending to conquer his own manhood and redeem his mother's soul?

Will the injurers ever forgive?

THE END.